MINE!

by
RACHEL
BRIGHT

PUFFIN

Allow me to introduce you to **Fifi**

and **Frankie**

....the twins.

Fifi's **best** things are ponies,

princesses and the colour pink.

Her **worst** thing is peas.

Frankie's **best** things are bears.

bicycling and the colour blue.

Her **worst** thing is bedtime.

But they both have the SAME bestest thing in the

whole

wide

world...

FUNNY BUNNY!

Their
favouritest
toy ever.

Frankie loves to take him on the teddy-bear express.

(no ponies allowed)

Wherever the twins go, Funny Bunny goes too.
Today they are visiting Grandma Flo.

"I'm holding Funny Bunny." Fifi **always** wants to hold him.

"No! I'm holding Funny Bunny." Frankie **always** wants to hold him too.

But, oh dear,
you've guessed it,
there's only **One**
Funny Bunny, so . . .

"AAAAAAAAAAAAAAA!
...You BROKE Funny Bunny!
WAAAAAAAA!
WAAAAAA
WAAAAAAAAAAAAAA

Funny Bunny couldn't believe
his not-there-any-more ears.

It was definitely
time to explain that
sometimes
you have to **share**.

And so, while Grandma Flo mended
Funny Bunny one ear at a time,
they worked something
out **together**.

And now
on Mondays

and

wednesdays

and **Fridays**, it's
Fifi's turn to play with
Funny Bunny.

Which is **ok** with **Frankie**, because on **Tuesdays**

and
Thursdays

and **Saturdays**, it's her turn to play with him.

And even though sharing isn't always easy . . .

...everybody

loves Sundays!

well...

...almost everybody.

For my lovely grandmas & incredible
grandads, with all my never-ending love

And with ginormous thank-yous to Robbie
& Elvis for unwavering loveliness & to the
fabulously talented Mandy & Rebecca & Goldy.

PUFFIN BOOKS
Published by the Penguin Group: London, New York, Australia,
Canada, India, Ireland, New Zealand and South Africa
Penguin Books Ltd, Registered Offices:
80 Strand, London WC2R 0RL, England

puffinbooks.com

First published 2011
006
Text and illustrations copyright © Rachel Bright, 2011
All rights reserved
The moral right of the author/illustrator has been asserted
Made and printed in China
ISBN: 978–0–141–33213–0

In loving memory of Leningrad (small cuddly dog) –
my favouritest toy ever . . . lost on a beach
(in Wales c. 1981) but not forgotten.